The Furricious

Gang SURREY

Of Godalming

Book 2

A children's book for grown ups

Martyn MacDonald Adams

1st Edition 2022

MMA Associates

ISBN-13: 978-1-7396924-6-9

Illustrations by Lisa Sacchi

Editor Alan Barker

DEDICATION

To my ex-wife and her stories of a naughty, flying bear and my darling daughter with a similar sense of zany humour.

CONTENTS

Humphrey, Jeffrey, and Godfrey

Woof's Birthday

It was a cosy, quiet, relaxed Sunday afternoon, when Jeffrey burst through the lounge door.

"You have to get something for Woof!"

Humphrey was lying on the long settee, with his feet toasting nicely against the curled-up body of Snowy, Godalming's very own white cat. She was purring in that way contented cats purr - a sort of cute snore-like buzzing. Humphrey looked up from reading his copy of the weekend's Urseta Times.

"So, I'm running errands for him now?" he asked.

"Are you? I suppose that would count."

"Count what?"

"Count as a birthday present."

Humphrey's eyes blinked at exactly the same time as Jeffrey would have heard the penny drop (had there been a penny dropping), as Humphrey realised what the conversation was really about.

One of Snowy's ears twitched.

"Ah! It's his birthday soon, is it?"

"Uhm," Jeffrey replied, slightly confused that Humphrey hadn't known this, and also slightly unsure if 'soon' was the right word.

"Have you got him anything?"

"A plastic chew-toy. A special one."

"Nice. Although I should imagine he has a few of those already. Where did you get it?"

"I bought it off the scribbles. They got it from a bin, I think."

"You've cleaned it up then?"

"Oh yes. It's spotless now. And I've put new batteries in it."

"Good. Good..." There was a short pause before Humphrey's eyes blinked again at exactly the same time that Jeffrey would have heard a penny dropping (had there been an actual penny dropping of course).

"...batteries?"

"Uhm," Jeffrey replied, nodding enthusiastically at the same time.

One of Snowy's ears twitched again and then pointed itself directly at Jeffrey, like a curious radar-dish. The other pointed itself at Humphrey.

"Can I see this... 'chew-toy'?" Humphrey folded his newspaper and sat up straight.

Jeffrey disappeared and ran back to his room, returning within seconds to show Humphrey his clever purchase.

"Ah..." said Humphrey. His eyebrows were jumping up and down, not knowing what position, under these particular circumstances, they should adopt. He sighed deeply. "Jeffrey...?"

Jeffrey looked at Humphrey with the sort of expression that only makes it more difficult to explain an awkward situation.

"This isn't, exactly, a 'chew-toy'."

Jeffrey's expression didn't change, but Snowy stopped purring, lifted her head, yawned, and stretched out before sitting up blinking while smacking her lips.

Humphrey sighed. "Oh dear. How can I explain this? This isn't really suitable to give to Woof as a birthday present."

"Why not?"

Snowy looked at Jeffrey before catching sight of the 'chew-toy'. She froze. Her eyes grew as wide as saucers and she started to grin. The tip of her tail flicked back and forth as if swatting at an invisible mosquito.

"This isn't a 'chew-toy'."

"But he could use it as one, couldn't he? Look, if you switch it on it makes a buzzing sound and wobbles."

Snowy held a paw in front of her mouth and suppressed a giggle.

"Yes. Yes, quite. You see, it's not the sort of thing that..."

"I bet he hasn't got one like that one!"

"No. No, I *bet* he hasn't. You see..." Humphrey scratched his head. How could he explain it to Jeffrey?

"Perhaps I should make it wobble-less? It might give him a headache if he chews on it for a long time."

"Yes. No. Let me explain... Jeffrey. You know how men and ladies both wear hats? But you wouldn't buy a lady bear's hat for a man bear?"

"Ye-es..." replied Jeffrey. "Because lady-bears wear silly hats with flowers on, but men-bears wear waterproof ones."

"Yes, like that immigrant from Peru. Well, this is a sort of 'chew-toy' that human ladies like to, erm, 'chew on'. Privately. In private. It's not really suitable for giving to male Woofs for their birthday. Do you see?"

"Why not? It's not got any flowers on it."

Snowy started to shake with suppressed laughter. Humphrey glanced at his feline companion and blushed.

"Because..." Humphrey's wool-based brain gave up. "Because it isn't!"

"But I've spent all my chocolate biscuits on it!"

"I know. I know. I'm sorry. Perhaps I could buy it off you for what you paid for it."

"Why do *you* want it? Do you want to chew on it? I want to keep it! It's cool. And it makes my teeth feel funny."

There was a short pause before Humphrey's eyes blinked again, at exactly the same time that Jeffrey would have heard yet another penny dropping (had there been - you know what I'm going to say. Perhaps teddy bears should come with a penny dropping device inside their head so one could tell when they've realised something. Anyway...)

"What? That does it! I'm going to have to dispose of this."

Snowy's face was now glowing with humour, but she remained diplomatically silent.

And so, for a while, it seemed to become very difficult for Humphrey to organise Woof's birthday presents.

Despite Humphrey giving Jeffrey no less than eighteen chocolate biscuits in compensation, Jeffrey continued to sulk and refused to talk. Furthermore, the third and youngest bear in the household, Godfrey, was his usual quiet self and living in a fairy-tale land of butterflies, unicorns, and current buns; but it was Godfrey's suggestion that suddenly made it all become much easier, if somewhat more complicated and expensive at the same time.

"Brilliant! We'll bake him a beetfruit cake from all of us."

Upon hearing this, their feline guest, who knew a lot about baking but a lot more about teddy bears, decided to go out on the prowl. Besides, she'd received a complaint from the Avian Musicians Union regarding certain younger members of Godalming's bird population who had elected to start rapping the early morning chorus instead of singing it. This was not traditional, and this was Godalming – in Surrey! Such behaviour simply would *not* do.

She checked her razor-sharp claws, before politely thanking the bears for a most amusing afternoon, and then departed their underground lair.

Humphrey went to the kitchen, put on his pink-flowered pinafore, and got another one for Godfrey who had elected to help him bake the cake.

"Okay," said Humphrey, reading from the cookbook. "First. Preheat the oven to three hundred and twenty degrees." He looked at the bears' old electric oven. It didn't have any markings on it. They'd rubbed off long ago when Jeffrey had enthusiastically cleaned it. "Well, there's three hundred and sixty degrees in a circle so I suppose that's almost all the way around."

"Second. Grease a cake pan." He fetched the closest thing he had: a dented old frying pan that had lost its handle when Jeffrey had enthusiastically cleaned that too, then he used it as a dinner gong.

"Third. Cream it with butter and sugar." Godfrey fetched the butter from the fridge and Humphrey cut a healthy chunk of it into the frying pan. Then both the bears set about tearing the small paper bags of sugar (teddy bears don't use much sugar - they tend to stock their shelves by surreptitiously acquiring it from various retail and coffee shops in Godalming High Street). Once they had a little heap, Godfrey started mixing it up with the butter using a wooden spoon. This wasn't easy as the butter was still cold and hard, and little Godfrey wasn't known for his culinary strength.

"Fourth. Add the eggs and vanilla..." Humphrey broke two eggs and put them in. Not having any vanilla, he dropped a vanilla choc-ice in from the freezer as the next best thing. This was also a good time to add some beetfruit, so he put some of that in after chopping it up.

"Fiveth. Stir in the cake flour." Uh oh. He rummaged through the cupboard and found some flour. It wasn't marked as 'cake flour' but it would do.

"Sixth. Boy! This is complicated. Pour the batter into the pan." He looked around for some batter. He was puzzled, though. Surely batter was what you did with fish and chips? Then he remembered – he had some battered fish in the freezer. He chipped the box of fish out of the ice, extracted the frozen fish, skinned the batter off it and added it to the mix before returning the now-naked fish to the freezer.

"Seventh. Bake the cake for an hour and fifteen minutes." He took the lumpy mess from Godfrey, noting that Godfrey had somehow managed to get some of the mixture onto his nose and ears. Using a knife, he chopped and mixed the contents a bit more (the choc-ice had melted far quicker than the butter, which was still lumpy). Then he put the lot into the oven.

"Thank you for your help, Godfrey," said Humphrey. "One birthday cake coming up!"

The cake didn't quite come out as expected. It certainly had not risen (which was just as well because the frying pan didn't have very tall sides). There was also something vaguely savoury about the crispy bits on top. But Humphrey was a clever and experienced bear, as feral teddy bears go, so he covered it with sprinkles and cream and put it in the fridge.

"Jelly," said Godfrey, and that one word was enough. Birthdays mean jelly, just as Christmas means Christmas trees, and Easter means chocolate Easter eggs. Teddy bears like jelly, and Humphrey had a lot of experience in making it. Soon the refrigerator was full of cake, cream, ice cream, and jelly.

When Jeffrey discovered that the fridge was full of jellies, cream, and sprinkles, his sulky mood evaporated, and like the enthusiastic bear he was, he joined the other two in helping to organise Woof's birthday. The three bears sat down and discussed what they could get Woof as a birthday present.

Godfrey's suggestions seemed to revolve around butterflies, unicorns, and current buns. Jeffrey's suggestions seemed to revolve around rocket packs, rocket-assisted bungee cords, and submersible speed boats - with built-in rocket packs.

During their last visit to Woof's 'bijou' tree residence, Humphrey noticed that the floors had seemed a little rough, damp, and musty. So, after some serious explaining, cajoling, and threatening, the two younger bears agreed to acquire some quality wood planking, glue, saws, nails, and hammers.

And so, when Woof called round to the bears' secret lair to deliver his weekly supply of beetfruit he was most surprised to see the dining room table laid out with jellies, chocolate biscuits, chocolate cakes, fairy cakes, a fizzling sparkler, and the words 'Hapy Bathday Wouf!' painted on an old bed sheet and draped across the dining room ceiling, only centimetres above the fizzling sparkler.

"Surprise!" called out the Furricious Gang.

"Yeow!" screamed Woof, seeing the word 'Bath' on the sign. He dropped his basket of beetfruit and was about to make a dash for the door, when his way was blocked by a manically grinning Jeffrey, holding a large dessert spoon in his paw.

Woof thought fast. Did he really smell that bad? The bears had never mentioned this before. Even Snowy, a very clean and clinical cat, had never mentioned anything about his personal hygiene. Furthermore, it was the end of October; the season of Halloween, witches, and monsters was coming soon. Maybe once a year, feral teddy bears suddenly became monsters and forcefully bathed all their friends.

Or maybe it was a full moon and the bears had suddenly become monstrous Woof-bathing were-bears.

His eyes wide with fear, Woof froze.

"Happy birthday Woof!" called out Godfrey.

"What?" Woof relaxed, realising what had happened. "That's not how you spell birthday." He sighed. Humphrey frowned, wondering how on earth Woof could tell how

10

Godfrey had spelt 'birthday' when saying 'Happy birthday Woof!' Could Woof see subtitles under the bears whenever they spoke?

"Besides," said Woof, "it's not my birthday for another month."

Humphrey looked at Jeffrey.

"I know," he said.

"You knew? You said it was Woof's birthday!"

"No, I didn't!"

"Yes, you did. You said I had to get him a birthday present!"

"But you do. For when it's Woof's birthday."

Humphrey slapped his forehead in an exasperated gesture of ursine frustration. "But we've made him a birthday cake and everything!"

"Yes," Jeffrey nodded. "I don't know why, but can I have a jelly now?"

And so, after the bears extinguished the sudden fire caused by the torn bed sheet falling on the fizzling sparkler, Woof and the Furricious Gang had a pre-birthday birthday party for Woof. A rehearsal, if you like. The jellies were a success, but the heavy beetfruit cake with fishy-flavoured crispy bits, and a coating of sprinkles and cream and extinguisher powder, didn't seem to be quite as popular as Humphrey had hoped.

Humphrey, Jeffrey and Godfrey

The Drone and the Secret Door

Humphrey woke up with a start, face down, his nose pressed against the dusty living- room carpet. He squinted briefly at the stiff, woolly pattern. It was out of focus and looked unreal.

"Where am I?" he muffumbled.

"On the carpet," answered a disembodied voice.

"Which one?"

"The one on the floor."

Only Jeffrey would answer that way.

It was early Sunday afternoon, not the time for an energetic response. Although, being a teddy bear, there never is a suitable time for an energetic response - unless of course there happens to be a flood, fire, or picnic involved. Humphrey didn't feel wet, couldn't sense any smoke, and couldn't smell any food, so he just lay there and took a moment to think. He remembered starting his Sunday afternoon nap then nothing more. He contemplated returning back to that land of sweet dreams. After all, he couldn't fall any further, could he?

Then again, it was Jeffrey who was standing behind him and that made him feel uneasy.

Then Godfrey chirped up, "You falled off the settee."

That decided it. Both of them together in the same room meant that no matter how lazy he felt, he'd just have to see what was going on otherwise there'd be no peace. He turned over, sat up, and rubbed his nose.

"How?"

"With a bump," said Jeffrey, helpful as ever. He was standing by the door with his paws behind his back.

"A big one," said Godfrey, nodding enthusiastically as if it was something to be proud of. "But you didn't bounce."

"But how?" demanded Humphrey.

"Well, gravity always pulls things down to the ground, like apples falling onto the top of Isaac Newton's hea..."

"I MEAN..." Humphrey took a deep breath and calmed himself before asking, "I mean, how was it that one moment I was peacefully dreaming of frilly pink pinafores, fur-lined handcuffs, warm custard, and wellington boots, and the next moment I'm French kissing Godfrey's dried milk stains on the carpet?"

Jeffrey's nose crinkled up. "Perhaps it was the stilton cheese you had after dinner? That always makes you dream funny."

Humphrey was about to explode in anger when Godfrey spoke up.

"It was an accin-dent." He pointed to a cushion in the far corner of the room.

Humphrey stared at it, recognising it as the one he'd been sleeping on earlier. He stood up and walked over to it. Lying underneath, and snagged by a pulled thread, was a four-engine remote control drone.

He glanced around the room and his eyes went wide when he saw his favourite nineteen-thirties period glass cabinet of ornaments lying on the floor. Thankfully none of the glass was broken, but some of the little knick-knacks and interesting items inside were. A little ornamental

Bambi now had a broken ear, and two glass horses had broken legs.

"Bambi!" Humphrey pointed at the unit. "Look at what you've done! We're going to have to visit the charity shop in the High Street again and get some more. You're paying for this!"

So, Jeffrey had acquired himself a toy, probably from one of those unruly scribbles. They seemed to delight in trading trouble with Jeffrey. He lifted the toy, disentangling it from the cushion.

"It's a really good drone," said Jeffrey. "It has a camera and a grappling hook."

"And it has a lady doctor too!" offered Godfrey, all wide-eyed and enthusiastic.

Humphrey and Jeffrey stopped, turned and frowned at the little bear.

"No," said Jeffery, "I said it has a GPS. That's not a lady doctor."

"Oh," answered Godfrey, slightly puzzled. "What do you call a lady doctor then?"

"Madam!" said Jeffrey, the self-declared fount of all ursine knowledge.

"Apart from throwing me off the settee and smashing my trinkets, what do you plan to do with this drone?"

"It's a business purchase. It will make me... uhm, us... a lot of biscuits."

Humphrey nodded. "Which means you're in debt to the scribbles now."

"But I can pay them back with what I make from the drone."

"I see. That's what they told you. And how does that work?"

"Well, the batteries power the motors which turn the blades very fast which pushes air downwards and makes the drone go upwards."

"...and it makes a loud vurring noise and it bumps into the walls and knocks pictures off the wall and hits the light bulbs and makes them go BANG! And then it goes all dark and it hits Jeffrey on the head and then he shouts rude words and then..."

"Godfrey!" yelled Jeffrey.

Humphrey slapped his forehead. This was turning out to be another 'one-of-them' days.

A plan of action crawled in Humphrey's fluff-based brain. First, confiscate the drone. Second, tour their underground cave-home and ascertain what damage this satanic device had done. But first...

"So, tell me, how does it help you pay back the debt... and pay for the damages you've done to our now-not-so-tidy-and-cute-little-hide-away home?"

Jeffrey stood stock still thinking furiously; but Godfrey had fewer life-preserving instincts.

"Jeffrey was going to fly it around Godalming at teatime and look for people having tea in their back gardins. Then he'd swoop down and grab their biscuits."

"I see."

Jeffrey was still thinking furiously – but from the look in his eyes the subject had changed. He was now almost certainly thinking along the lines of ursine-fratricide (that's murdering brother bears).

Humphrey, without taking his eyes off Jeffrey, pointed out, "Wouldn't the irate residents of... of this sweet little town, trace the drone back to its source? And then proceed to lynch us?"

There was a moment's silence until he answered his own question. "We could do it in Farncombe, I suppose..." He thought a little more. "And it would have to cross the river... to prevent people from chasing it... and it doesn't always have to be just biscuits. Chocolate cakes would do just as well. Even better maybe." Humphrey sat down and pondered the plan. It seemed to have potential. His ears started to stiffen ever so slightly.

The Furricious Gang could become the Notorious Godalming Picnic Sky-Jacking Gang. That had a devilish appeal to it. He grinned.

At that moment Snowy, Godalming's snow-white feline-of-the-flagpole, entered the room with her usual ghost-like elegance. She gingerly stepped over the fallen cabinet and glided up to the drone. The three bears watched as she sniffed at it, batted it with a paw once or twice, and then sat down.

Keeping their attention, she gracefully licked a paw, then said, "Don't underestimate humans. If you steal from them, they'll soon find you."

Humphrey sighed. She was right, as always. He'd seen the police helicopters hovering overhead (when the government could afford the petrol). It wouldn't take much for the pilot to dangle another policeman on a fishing line, who, holding a net, could then capture the drone and replace the chocolate cake with a homing beacon. Then where would they be?

He seriously doubted that he could bribe the Surrey Constabulary with a percentage of the takings. They ate a *lot* of cake, apparently. Or so he'd heard.

"Mouse trafficking. Now *that* has potential." She continued to lick her paws.

"You mean we could fly mice from one side of the river to the other? Like a taxi service. A miniature airline." Humphrey's ears stiffened again at the thought of a profitable, and not quite so risky, enterprise. "We could also handle shrews, and maybe even squirrels. We could sell them holiday packages... rent them holiday nests..."

"Yes. And naturally I'd like a percentage."

"Of the fares?"

"Of the mice. Silly bear!" she sighed.

"Ah!" Humphrey's ears flopped again. He wasn't having any of that. There was something unethical about animal trafficking and bears didn't do anything unethical (which is why they make such poor politicians. Also, teddy bears tend to 'selectively think' a lot, which is why Humphrey had already forgotten about Jeffrey's idea of sky-napping chocolate cakes – which certainly *would* seem to be unethical to the person looking forward to a tea party only to have their favourite cake snatched away by a remote-controlled drone).

Humphrey decided to change the subject. "Did you manage to catch it?"

Snowy looked quizzical.

18

"You know, the culprit responsible for making Godalming's dawn chorus somewhat reggae-ish."

Her eyes narrowed.

Humphrey started singing, swaying, and clicking his thumbs on the off-beat.

Singin' don't worry...
'bout a thing
'Cause every little thing gonna be alright

"Ah yes. I remember now. It was a parrot. Some human must have let it escape. The Avian Musician's Union were most upset. Next thing you know, they'll be playing steel drums, drinking rum, and chillin'. Can't have that. Not in Godalming."

"How did you find it?"

"Tasty," she replied, with that innocent expression that only homicidal cats can carry off while still looking cute.

"Oh," said Humphrey, instantly regretting his question. He wondered if she had a similar licence to James Bond's, but one issued by the Avian Musicians Union.

Although, come to think of it, James Bond rarely ate his victims.

"Can I have my drone back?" asked Jeffrey.

"No. Not until I see what damage it has done." And with that he grabbed the young bear by an ear and marched him into the hall. "Now, show me what devilish damage that dastardly demonic device has done."

"Ow! Ow! Ow!" said Jeffrey.

Godfrey followed behind.

Humphrey let Jeffrey's ear go and raised an eyebrow.

"Well?"

"It didn't do that much damage really. Godfrey was exaggerating. Follow me." He led the other two down to the bedrooms while he rubbed at his pulled ear.

Outside Jeffrey's bedroom door Humphrey noticed scratches on the hallway wall and a dent in the paintwork.

"Are you responsible for this?"

"Uhm... No? It was the drone."

"And the broken light?"

"The drone."

"The dent in the ceiling?"

"Uhm... The drone?" Jeffrey was starting to feel uncomfortable.

Humphrey glanced around and saw an even worse crash site.

"And that?"

Jeffrey didn't want to nod. He bit his lip instead.

Something caught Humphrey's eye and he peered closer to the damage.

"That's funny," he whispered. "This plaster is covering a doorway."

He started peeling away at the wall. After a moment all three bears were pulling at the thick plaster to uncover a wooden door.

"I wonder what this is," whispered Humphrey, standing back.

"It's a secret door," said Jeffrey, helpful as ever.

"I know that! I wonder where it leads?"

Jeffrey, always knowledgeable about such things, stood beside Humphrey. "It could lead to a burial chamber. Maybe our ancestors are buried in it. Maybe it's got ghosts."

Godfrey immediately stopped peeling the paint and took a step back too. "I don't like goats."

"Oh, don't worry. If they're our ancestors then they'll be friendly. On the other hand, they might be the ghosts of the demons that killed our ancestors. Then they won't."

"They have horns," said Godfrey. "And long noses. And little legs. And scraggly hair. They eat your sandwiniches, and they bash you."

"Do they?" Jeffrey was a little surprised that Godfrey knew so much about these ancestor-killing demons. Consequently, in his teddy-bear-mind's logic, they immediately became a historical fact, and this explained where all his ancestors had gone. They had all been murdered by short-legged, scraggly-haired, demonic forces.

"And they smell funny," said Godfrey, now afraid that he'd be trampled and butted by a herd of crazed goats.

But Humphrey had been thinking along different lines.

"I wonder if it's a secret room filled with treasure. A treasure chamber." He felt his ears stiffen again. "There was a rumour about Great-Uncle Alfred having a secret stash of something."

Humphrey and Jeffrey peeled away the remaining plaster until the door was completely uncovered. Humphrey squinted at the lock beside the hole where the door handle had once lived.

"I wonder how we can open it."

"We could hit it with a hammer," suggested Jeffrey.

"Don't hit it with a ham-ner! You'll wake up the goats!" Godfrey sounded upset.

"It could be full of treasure. Boxes of chocolate digestive biscuits stacked from floor to ceiling." Humphrey was now getting quite excited. "Or even, money. Or even better... a stack of picnic baskets filled with picnics and chocolate hobnobs."

Godfrey was more sceptical. "The goats would have eatened them," he sighed.

"But as soon as we open the door we'll know!" said Humphrey, his mind now considering what he'd do with a thousand custard tarts, and his ears now quite rigid.

Godfrey's mouth dropped open. He turned and ran away, towards the kitchen.

"What about the ghosts?" asked Jeffrey.

"Demons, spirits, and ghosts can all walk through walls. They would have been here already. They don't like picnics either. No, we don't have to worry about ghosts, just how to open this door."

Jeffrey wasn't too sure. Evidently, they'd already killed his ancestors. This must therefore be a trap. He turned and ran into his bedroom.

Humphrey stood there alone and a little surprised. He knew the other two were un-brave – that was natural (teddy bears are not cowards, but are not always brave either) – but he hadn't expected them to run away. He heard shuffling sounds from Jeffrey's room and clanging noises from the kitchen. His mind wandered back to imagining

Great-Uncle Alfred's treasure. Boxes of fairy cakes, cheesecakes, angel cakes, Battenberg cakes, pickled onion cakes, and...

He snapped out of his reverie and looked again at the door.

It looked strong.

It also looked as if it knew it was strong and it also knew that Humphrey would make himself look foolish after he'd failed to open it. Now it looked smug.

Humphrey decided he didn't like this door. It was being greedy, hiding all those wonderful things. Keeping them all to itself.

As Humphrey pondered the door, Jeffrey and Godfrey returned to his side. Jeffrey was now wearing his homemade batman, or rather bat-bear, costume – but the bat ears were large and rounded, and the nose guard was quite large giving him an appearance that was closer to a navy-blue Mickey Mouse than a fearsome caped crusader. Humphrey didn't want to say anything but he strongly suspected his dyed bedsheet cape was fraying at the neck and wouldn't last long. And the bright yellow wellington boots just looked wrong.

Godfrey had, quite intelligently, armoured himself up in the kitchen. He had acquired a large saucepan on his head (which had to be held up by the handle so he could see where he was going). He'd tied a saucepan lid to his tummy and another to his back, and in his paws he held a large wooden spoon ready to donk the first goat that came out of that door.

"Dressed for the occasion, I see," remarked Humphrey.

"I've got my bat-belt on," said Jeffrey. "It's got a pen-knife, old batteries, a TV remote control that doesn't work anymore, some old rusty keys, a slingshot, some mains wire, and lots of other stuff."

"Wonderful. I'm sure they'll be very useful against the ghosts." For a moment Humphrey wondered what went on in Jeffrey's bear/bat/mouse mind. "I also notice you've recently dyed your bat-pants, but that they haven't dried yet. I suspect you'll look like you're still wearing bat-bear's blue briefs even after you've taken them off. Our fur takes to dye quite nicely. I dread to think what new colours your bat-bear blue bedsheets are going to be tomorrow morning."

Godfrey felt quite pleased with himself. He was alright. He was armoured, and those head-butting goats couldn't hurt him now. Even with their horns and short legs.

Snowy, having been abandoned in the lounge, had decided to come down the hall and see what the bears were up to. She sat down, cocked her head sideways, first one way, then the other, and took in the scene from all angles.

Humphrey turned his attention back to the door and squinted into the lock. An idea sprang into his head.

"Jeffrey. You don't happen to have those bat-bear-keys of yours handy, do you?"

"Oh yes!" Jeffrey struggled with his bat-bear-belt utility pack and in the end had to take it off and pry it open to reveal a set of rusty keys. He handed them over to Humphrey.

"Thank you." Humphrey tried each one in turn but none fitted the door.

"Is it locked?" asked Snowy.

"What?"

24

"The door."

"I think so," said Humphrey. But there was something about the tone of Snowy's voice…

"Have you tried it?"

"None of the keys fit."

She sighed. "Have you tried just opening the door with your paw?"

Then it hit him like a flying brick of fluff, feathers, and fur. "Ah. No. But that was going to be my next idea."

Gingerly, Humphrey took hold of the hole where the door handle used to be, and pulled. The door creaked open...

An ancient ironing board, folded flat and standing upright, fell forward and struck Humphrey on the head. With lightning, self-preserving bat-bear reactions Jeffrey leapt backwards out of the way and struck his head on the opposite wall. He fell to the floor, stunned.

Godfrey, prepared for the attack of a rabid herd of goats, leapt forward and donked the ironing board as hard as he could with his wooden spoon before falling over backwards. Humphrey lay double-dazed under the ironing board.

Snowy's head did that cute puzzled-cat thing where the head rotates ninety degrees to one side, and then to the other. She frowned, sighed, and started licking at her paw. Bears!

Humphrey staggered up from beneath the ironing board and, holding his head, peered into the secret room. Save for an empty matchbox, it was empty.

Godfrey sat up. "Where did the goats go?"

Jeffrey, still dazed, sat up. "Can I have my drone now?"

The response from Humphrey was un-bear-able.

Humphrey, Jeffrey and Godfrey

The Hair Cut

"So, how would you like me to trim it?"

Humphrey felt a little uneasy sitting under a thick blanket on a highchair in Woof's tree house. He stared into the mirror at, what seemed to him, a maniacal dog-barber about to decapitate an innocent teddy bear with a pair of scissors. He started to regret accepting his friend's offer to make him look sexier.

Woof snipped eagerly at the air.

"Err, a little off the top, a little off the sides and off the collar. Just tidy it up."

Woof nodded. "And the other ear?"

(Snip, snip)

"Ear? Are you hinting I've got hairy ears?"

"Nooooo. No, no, no. Not hinting at all. I'm telling you; your ears *are* hairy."

(Snip, snip, snip)

Humphrey sighed. Woof was, in fact, correct. Then again, all teddy bears have hairy ears. His had been just a little more 'enthusiastic' in that department recently.

"Yours are worse!" Humphrey grumbled back, and winced as Woof continued to snip away at nothing in particular.

(Snip, snip, snip)

"Ah, but woofs like me are considered handsome if we have thick, hairy ears." And so, he started trimming the bear's flappy bits. A split second after each snip Humphrey's ear would twitch involuntarily but Woof soon got into the rhythm of things, and slowly but surely, they were neatly trimmed.

The would-be barber then moved on to tidy up the rest of the teddy bear's head and then gently trim his eyebrows. It didn't take long, for although Humphrey was hairy, it was teddy-bear hair and it never grew too long or too wild. Not for Humphrey anyway, but he knew that female teddy bears could be much more critical.

Earlier in the week, Woof had been trotting down Godalming's High Street when he'd seen the local barbers at work in their shop. He'd sat outside and watched, fascinated by the skill of the hairdressers. Now he wanted to try out this new knowledge on someone and a teddy bear in need of a tidy up was a perfect candidate.

"I think I need to tackle those small, difficult-to-cut, fuzzy hairs," said Woof, peering inside Humphrey's left ear. He put down his scissors, reached to one side and produced a short metal rod with a cotton tip. Then, he opened a small metal bottle of something and dipped the tip of the rod inside, before deftly striking a match and lighting the end. Humphrey's eyebrows rose a little in surprise. Woof then gently whapped the side of Humphrey's ear with the fiery

tip and a small, crinkly flame shot up and instantly
vanished.

In one instant he'd eradicated all those little hairs that
are too bothersome to trim.

It happened so fast that Humphrey didn't have time to scream. But now his left ear was warm. Very warm, but also quite comfy-warm. Outwardly, he was still halfway toward full-blown panic, with eyes and mouth making large O shapes. As he paused to ponder this event Woof whapped the other ear, and another crinkly flame shot up and vanished. Humphrey now had two very, very warm ears and two very, very close brushes with a fiery demise.

On the plus side, not one of those all-but-invisible hairs remained.

"Are you trying to set me on fire?"

"Don't be silly. I saw the barbers in the High Street do it – although, come to think of it, when *they* do it there's no sheet of flame."

"You don't say!"

"If you let those little hairs grow again, I reckon that would be a neat trick for fireworks night. Don't you think?"

"No, it wouldn't! Stop it!"

Woof examined Humphrey's nose.

"Do you have hairy nostrils?"

"No! Look, I came here for a trimming, not a toasting. What would you have done if I had caught fire?"

"Oh, don't worry. My little tree house would be just fine. That's a fire blanket you're wearing. You see? I thought of everything. I even have a bucket of water beside us, just in case."

"Oh," said Humphrey.

"So, tell me, what's all this trimming for? You have a date with a lady bear perhaps?"

"Family visit."

"Product?"

"Prod who?"

"Would sir like some product? I don't have much to offer but I have a fresh air spray, a jelly in the fridge, and maybe a jar of Vaseline somewhere."

"Fresh hair sounds good. Thanks."

Woof went to the lavatory and returned with a spray can.

"When you said fresh..."

Woof sprayed at Humphrey's head.

"...Ah ...ah ...ahtchoo!"

"There you are, smelling like a pile of clean linen. Just like my nice clean lavatory. Hot towel?"

"I'be dod wed."

"Pardon?"

"I'be dot wet!"

"You're not wet. No, but my mirror is," said Woof, peering at the spatter on his mirror. "I'll have to clean it now. The next time I trim you, remind me to fit a windscreen wiper on my mirror first. By the way, the kettle is boiled, and the hot towel is steamed. It feels wonderful. It opens your pores. Would you like to try it...?"

"My paws are fine, thanks."

In fact, Humphrey's paws were still clenching the arms of the chair from the whapping.

Woof held up a hand mirror so that the bear could see the back of his head. Thankfully it looked pretty much as it did before. No sign of singed hair.

"How much do I owe you?" asked Humphrey as he clambered down to the floor making a silent resolution never to do this again.

"Three will do."

Humphrey handed over three chocolate biscuits, then broke a chocolate bourbon in half and gave it to Woof as a tip. He ate the other half, mainly to calm his nerves.

"Thank you," smiled Woof and put them into his new biscuit tin, making a quiet "Kerching!" sound to himself.

It was raining outside, so Humphrey put his child-face mask on, the one that, from a distance, and to a very short-sighted person, made him *almost* look like a very young human, albeit one with a big nose. He then grabbed his child's plastic raincoat, put the hood up, and pulled on his miniature bright red wellingtons. Basically, he'd copied the idea from an illegal immigrant from Peru, but the face mask was all his. The number of opticians in Godalming's High Street was testimony as to how short-sighted the locals were.

He bid Woof a hearty farewell, and set off along the river path toward his secret home under Godalming's bowling clubhouse, which no-one, except those with special knowledge, knew anything about.

Humphrey would never admit it, but he loved the rain, and being dressed as a child was a really good excuse to stamp in all the puddles along the way. Not everything humans did was silly. In his view, the older humans got, the sillier they became. It was the older ones that had invented silly things like mortgage repayments, wars, and parking tickets. He wondered why they thought they were so intelligent.

But, to his surprise, he found himself already missing that cosy-warm-ear feeling. It had been a really, really nice feeling. So much so, he wondered when he'd have the courage to live dangerously and have another one of Woof's haircuts. Fireworks night maybe?

Provided Woof had a bucket of water nearby. A big one.

Humphrey, Jeffrey and Godfrey

The Inheritance

Early one morning, there was a knock on the front door.

"They're here!" yelled Humphrey, from the kitchen, as he removed his pink floral pinafore.

There was a rumble along the hallway and a 'boink!' sound as Godfrey dashed out of his room, faster than his legs could cope, bumped into the front door and hurtled backwards to land flat on his back.

"Ow!" he said, rubbing his nose.

"So now we know. Little bears' noses are *very* bouncy," said Humphrey. He glanced down the hall to see Jeffrey dragging himself reluctantly toward them.

"But I suspect we'll have much longer to wait to find out if larger ones are just as squishable."

Humphrey pulled open the front door. In front of him stood three female bears, in descending order of height: Bernadette, Colette, and little Yvette.

"Hello. Humphrey?"

"Hello Bernadette. Girls," replied Humphrey. "We've been expecting you. Do come in."

The girls entered the gang's home and took off their damp coats (it was raining outside). Humphrey passed them over to Godfrey, as he showed the girls into the living room. Godfrey staggered back towards his bedroom but didn't make it, falling over and dumping their wet clothes on the floor. As it happened this was a good thing because the hall was in need of a clean.

In the living room, Humphrey tried his best at being sociable, but sadly, this was not one of his best skills. Besides, he was secretly afraid of Bernadette; she could be so bossy. She always made him nervous therefore he'd prepared for their arrival by committing the list of conversational subjects to his wool-based brain.

"Please, ladies. Take a seat. You must be Colette and Yvette. Did you have a nice journey? I do like your dress. Can I get you a cup of tea? How are you keeping? What pretty earrings. Have you had your holidays yet? Are you warm enough? It's been such a long time. Would you like some biscuits? Isn't the weather just appropriate, or not? Should I turn up the heating? How is Aunty Florrie? Would you prefer milk or orange juice? Let me turn up the heating." Humphrey, having now exhausted all his icebreakers in less than fifteen seconds, ran out of the room to turn up the heating. He congratulated himself on remembering them all, and all in the right order too.

Yay!

Godfrey dodged the triumphant bear as he flew past and peered around the living room door.

"Hullo," he said.

"Hullo," said little Yvette. The smallest of the three.

"I've got a colouring book," said Godfrey, who then turned around and left. Yvette, without any prompting, got down from the chair and followed him to his room. Within just a few seconds they had both settled down and were colouring in scenes of animals in the woods, marine creatures in the sea, and birds pooing on the cars parked in Godalming's various town centre car parks.

At their age, six words are enough. A skill completely lost on human politicians.

Jeffrey hung about outside the door wondering what to do, what to say, and how to say it, when Humphrey arrived with a tray of several cups and saucers, a tea pot, a sugar bowl, and some biscuits.

"Come on in and say hello," said Humphrey.

"Do I have to?"

"Yes. They are your cousins and they've come to visit us for the day. You have to say hello. There are rules."

"Can't you say it for me?"

"Oh, for goodness' sake! Open the door and go in."

Humphrey followed Jeffrey into the living room and placed the tea tray on the coffee table. He stopped and thought for a moment. "Is it right to put tea on a coffee table? It seems wrong somehow."

"Perfectly all right." Bernadette smiled. "And to answer your questions... yes, yes, and yes. Thank you. That would be nice. Fine. Thank you. No. Yes, thank you. Indeed. The girls might enjoy them. Isn't it? There's absolutely no need, and she's fine. The girls might prefer them and really, there is no need."

Humphrey was now aware that the entire morning's conversation had been completed in just a few minutes, but he took solace in the thought that having muffed up the first round, they could start again from the top and this would fill in even *more* time. So, in point of fact, this had proved to be a brilliant conversational tactic. He made a mental note for next time.

"Here is Jeffrey. Say hello, Jeffrey."

"Hello, Jeffrey," mumbled Jeffrey, staring down at the carpet.

"We seem to be missing some bears."

Bernadette smiled. "Godfrey and Yvette have already made friends and have gone to play." She turned to Jeffrey. "My, my. How you have grown. You are a big handsome bear now. Perhaps you would like to show Collie around?"

Jeffrey perked up. There was a dog here? Where? Then he realised Bernadette was referring to Colette and his face dropped.

"Uh."

Humphrey stepped up. "Show Colette your laboratory and workshops. I'm sure she'd be interested in your nuclear-powered, bungee-assisted, high-altitude sandwich delivery device."

"Uh. It's supposed to be a secret."

"That's alright, Jeffrey. We're all family here. Besides, it's a good idea." Humphrey turned to Bernadette. "It's a new scheme of Jeffrey's. We could make money by making freshly-made sandwiches to order and delivering them to airliners as they pass overhead."

"...and anyway..." mumbled Jeffrey.

"What?"

"She's a girl."

Dark indignation swept over Colette's face, as if she were a Trump mistaken for an Obama. Her voice could have cracked windows (if not skulls): "So, I suppose that, in your view, being 'a girl' means I know nothing about managing the fluctuating core temperature so as to ensure that fatigue stresses on reactor coolant pipes do not lead to premature cracking?"

There was a pause which, if it could have been bottled, would have made an excellent paint stripper.

Jeffrey stood frozen while his brain recovered from what was, evidently, a major, *major,* miscalculation. After his brain-reset, his opinion of his cousin had been completely revisited, reviewed, revoked, and revised.

Besides, she had this cute little flower pinned to her dress...

He beckoned to her. "It's this way."

She rose from her chair and followed him out of the room, the atmosphere palpably cooling as they left. From the corridor, Humphrey heard her ask, "How do you manage the recoil from the bungee cords? I've even tried using multiple Velcro stacks, but..." Her voice faded into the distance.

"Well..." said Bernadette after they'd gone. "Shall I be Mother?"

"Oh. Do you think that's wise? After all, we're closely related and the children..."

"No, you daft bear! Shall I pour the tea?"

"Oh. Oh! Oh, yes. Sorry. Sorry! Oh dear... I didn't mean..."

"The reason I came, apart from being sociable, is to discuss Aunt Bessie's departure and her legacy."

"Where is she going? What's wrong with her leg...?" Humphrey knew immediately that he'd misheard and/or misunderstood Bernadette by the exasperated look on her face.

"She died, Humphrey. She's dead. She has since ceased to share, care, or swear. She whoofs her custard no more. She no longer drinks spirits but, alas, is now one. I'm here to talk about her estate."

"Was it her leg that killed her?"

"Pardon? What on earth are you wittering about?"

"Ah! Sorry. When you said '...Aunt Bessie's departure and her leg you see...' I thought..." His voice tailed off. Humphrey thought furiously. She didn't have any land and didn't own an estate car as far as he could recall. Besides, how could a gammy leg kill someone? Unless someone had pulled it off and hit her over the head with it.

Bernadette huffed impatiently. Then, "Her estate, Humphrey. What remains in her will?"

"Oh! Yes. Sorry."

So, perhaps he was wrong. Perhaps she did own land, or a car, and have a bad leg. And who was Will? Her new toy boy? He didn't want to sound too stupid, so he thought he'd listen on. Besides, she looked irritated and, when it came to Bernadette, Humphrey was not a brave bear.

"As you know, Bessie was very keen on painting. She painted a lot. An awful lot. A lot of awful paintings in fact. She left explicit instructions that these paintings were to be kept as family heirlooms and be preserved for future generations such that they may be enjoyed in the decades to come. It was her last wish that they must be displayed in a gallery for all eternity."

"I seem to remember her painting goats in yellow sou'westers and wellington boots. Is that what you mean?"

"Yes. Goats in raincoats, sou'westers, anoraks, t-shirts, skiing outfits, pink frilly tutus, short sexy kilts, nylon stockings, sheer mankinis, and goodness knows what else. All in the worst possible taste, and none of them in perspective either."

"Oh dear. How many of them are there?"

"Dozens," she replied flatly. "I promise you, the image of a goat wearing a floral baby-doll nighty and looking seductively over her shoulder will haunt you for the rest of your life." She shuddered.

"Oh dear."

"Yes. 'Oh dear', indeed. We need somewhere to display them indefinitely, preferably in an underground-sealed vault. And it was noted that your gang lives in an extensive underground maze of tunnels and rooms. Perhaps you could house them for us?"

Humphrey pondered the task.

"What's in it for me?"

She sipped calmly at her tea. "Twenty packets of various chocolate biscuits, including at least one, maybe more, of your favourites. What do you say?"

"Deal!"

"Wonderful! I shall let the others know. Now then, there's one other item that I need to resolve before you give me your usual boring tour of your home, chat about not-dogs who live in trees, and Godalming's green river monster."

Humphrey nodded, not paying attention. In his mind he was trying to sort out what needed to be moved in the kitchen cupboards to make room for this wonderful new treasure.

"She left you a small inheritance too."

"She did?" Humphrey's ears perked up and stiffened in expectation.

"Yes. But you have already agreed to accept those twenty packets of various chocolate biscuits, including at least one, maybe more, of your favourites. Have you not?"

"Uhm, yes?"

"Good. It is settled then. We are in agreement. Now tell me about Godfrey, Jeffrey, that cat, and those pesky squirrel-like scribbles. What have they been up to?" She sipped her tea.

Something in Humphrey's brain felt that something was amiss. It was as if he'd been given a puzzle but one of the pieces didn't quite fit.

On the other hand, twenty packets of biscuits wasn't to be sneezed at. Chocolate biscuits, no less. He was rich!

...But was that payment or was that inheritance?

Who cares! Twenty packets of chocolate biscuits! Yay!

***

Should you ever come to Godalming and manage to take a tour of Humphrey, Jeffrey, and Godfrey's home, you will find, to your surprise, that deep underground there is a small art gallery. One that the Furricious Gang never visits, well at least not on purpose, and would prefer not to visit at all. However, even more surprisingly, every now and then, a delegation of reverential scribbles come from far and wide to pay a small fee (in chocolate biscuits of course) to admire those secret, sobering, and sometimes 'provocative' works of capricious art.

Humphrey, Jeffrey and Godfrey

The Flood

"Humpy! Humpy! Humpy! I can't get to sleep."

Humphrey tried to turn over, but his right ear refused to let him.

"Humpy! Humpy! Humpy! I can't get to sleep."

The voice interrupted Humphrey's dream of eating a roast lamb dinner with oodles of gravy, crispy roast potatoes, a steamed cauliflower covered in lemon sorbet, curried carrots, and baked beans with bacon-flavoured ice cream. All served up on a very large, very soft, chocolate digestive marshmallow. He opened one eye, half hoping for the Yorkshire pudding and custard dessert, but not only was he chewing the corner of his pillow, someone was pulling hard on his right ear.

That's when he saw the silhouette of the little teddy bear standing over him.

"Phwu! Phwu! Curried carrots? Wha... what time is it?" said the slightly less little and significantly older bear.

"I don't know, but I can't sleep."

For a moment Humphrey imagined that he had been fully awake at the dinner table and only now was he just dropping into a surreal dream. He glanced at the clock on the bedside table. It displayed **03:23**.

"It's night-time. Go to bed."

"I can't."

Humphrey pulled himself up and rubbed his eyes. "Uh! Why not?"

"It's raining."

"It's been raining for days. Go to bed." He rubbed his nose and sniffed.

"Awww. But I don't want to."

"Why not? Do you want to snuggle up next to me?" He rubbed his ears.

"Yes please!" And with that, Godfrey jumped under the covers beside Humphrey.

Squish!

"Wha... Wha... You're all wet! Yeuch! Get out!"

"Awww. I don't want to."

"Why are you all wet?"

"Because of the rain."

"It's been raining for days..." Humphrey paused. Apart from the steamed cauliflower covered in lemon sorbet, there was something else amiss here. "Have you been outside?"

"No."

"Why not?"

"It's raining."

Humphrey decided that it was most important to get this little bear dry and back into his own bed. Besides, he wanted to know more about the baked bean and bacon-flavoured ice cream. With great patience he got up, sighed, put his favourite pink bunny slippers on then led Godfrey, by his paw, back to his bedroom. He opened the door.

It was raining.

"See? I told you. It's raining."

"It shouldn't be raining *in* your bedroom, Godfrey. We live underground, under another building. The roof is waterproof. Unless..." A cold shiver ran down his spine.

Or it might have been a big drip from the ceiling.

Humphrey rushed into the living room and made a dash for the periscope. There was no view of the bowling green above; it was black outside, but then, at this time of night that was to be expected. He threw a switch, and the outside spotlight came on. The scene that drifted across the eyepiece looked like leafy bits of mint sauce dissolved in a dark, misty brown gravy, but from the dinner plate's point of view. There was no sign of the hedge and grass that should have been there. A twig drifted past the field of view, pretending to be a cartwheeling balloon. Then a big, round, silver eye appeared and stared back at Humphrey.

Surprised, the bear stood back, then stepped forward and looked again. It was a fish's eye alright. As it drifted away from the periscope, he could see the expression on its face. It was one of triumph. Fish-kind had arrived and were finally taking over the world.

The fish tried to wink at the stunned bear, but not having any eyelids it completely failed to do so. It swam off in a bit of a huff. Evolution had much to answer for – not just eyelids but other bits like ears, legs, fingers, and stuff. However, with the rise of the New Piscine Empire, all that malarkey had been rendered irrelevant and there was much new territory for it to explore. The town of Godalming was being reclaimed in the glorious name of 'Fish-Kind', although he wasn't sure what the new name for this territory was to be yet. Perhaps something nautical like Godder Bank?

Humphrey thought quickly.

"We're under water. We've got to waterproof your room. And quickly, before we are flooded too. Let's get to the basement and see what we can use."

As Humphrey turned, he saw Jeffrey standing at the lounge door, dripping on the floor, wearing a diver's face mask and snorkel.

"Is it raining in your bedroom too?" ventured the bear-in-charge, dreading the answer.

Jeffrey shook his head, spraying them a little. He removed the snorkel.

"No, but the basement is full of water. It's very cold and there's not much light down there."

Humphrey barged past the two younger bears and ran down the corridor to the basement steps. Water had nearly reached the top.

"Oh no. We're completely flooded. It's like we're sinking."

"It's a bit like we're in a submarine, and we've been depth charged, and the water is pouring in, and some of the crew are trapped and drowning, but we can't hear their screams, and we're sinking down to the bottom of the sea where we will be crushed by the water pressure. Squish!" Jeffrey made a squishing motion with his paws.

"What songs?" asked Godfrey.

"Songs?"

"You said we'll be singing to the bottom of the sea."

"Sinking, I said sinking. But you can sing if you want."

"Oh good. I like snubmanrines."

"Ha, ha! 'Snub-manrines'," cried out Jeffrey, pointing to the youngest bear.

Humphrey interjected. "Look, guys. We have a problem. I suggest we abandon ship and float to the surface in my... uhm... our... emergency life-boat-ball."

"But we're in a snubmanrine!" Godfrey was a little upset and quite keen on this new game. He'd never played this one before.

"Well, teddy bears don't do well underwater. We really do need to escape."

Humphrey led them to his bedroom where he had installed an emergency escape hatch above the top of one of his wardrobes. He pulled out a very large transparent, but deflated, beach ball and placed it on the bed.

"Climb inside this and I'll open the escape hatch, and we'll bob to the surface when the room floods." He stuffed his bath towel into the ball.

"But I want to play snubmanrines," howled Godfrey.

Jeffrey pulled himself inside the ball and reached out to the little bear.

"Come on. We can play shipwreck survivors instead."

"Not snubmanrines?"

"No, but we can be sailors that escaped from a sinking snub... submarine, and we can drift for days in the open ocean under the beating sun. We can be dying from thirst and hunger, and after we've eaten all the biscuits, we can decide which one of Humphrey's legs to eat first."

"The biscuits!"

If a dark brown bear could turn pale, Humphrey would have done so. He ran to the kitchen in a blind panic and reached for his store of nibblers. He opened the tin. "Phew!" he sighed, before grabbing a bottle of water, running back to the bedroom and tossing them into the ball.

Then he was off again, to the lounge. The water now saturated the carpets, so Humphrey's feet made splatting noises as he ran. He reached behind the settee for his secret stash of sugary shortbreads and then ran back to the bedroom and tossed them into the ball with the other two bears – but both had dark brown stains around their mouths.

"Stop eating the biscuits! They're for emergencies only."

"This *is* an emergency," declared Jeffrey, slowly raising a half-eaten digestive to his mouth.

"Yes. But save them. We'll need them for later, when we're hungry."

"But I'm hungry now," said Godfrey.

"Save them for later!" Humphrey ordered, "...and save some for me."

He turned, grabbed a key ring from beside his bed and ran to where he'd hidden his other secret biscuit stash, in his private secret safe, in his secret hidey-hole, in the locked hallway cupboard. By the time he got there the water was over the carpet and his pink bunny slippers were now making splishing sounds. Water was now dribbling down the walls from the ceiling.

He unlocked the cupboard and dodged the falling ironing board (which always tried its hardest to land on something soft, usually Humphrey's head). Humphrey then tugged open the secret door to his hidey-hole and turned the little wheels on the front of the safe. It sprang open.

Humphrey crinkled his nose in horror.

In the safe was a single, used, smelly sock, a broken plastic ray gun, a small glass jar of yellow powder labelled 'Yellow Cake Powwder. Doent Bake. Tastes Bad', a small brick of light grey marzipan labelled 'C4 – Doent Bash!', a small box of pills labelled 'Morning After', and a small dark bottle of liquid labelled 'Hydrazine - Save For Guy Fork's Knite.'

It was the box of pills that rattled Humphrey the most.

Clearly Jeffrey had discovered the safe, broken into it, and claimed it as his own. But after some blind rummaging around, Humphrey was relieved to find that his now not-so-secret slush fund – the stash of biscuits – was still intact at the back of the safe. It then occurred to him that the safe was watertight so there was in fact no reason whatsoever to rescue any of it. It was safer where it was, especially when he remembered that three bears floating in an enclosed ball with nothing to do but eat biscuits was not at all a good place to preserve his retirement fund.

And Jeffrey's items might need reviewing after this crisis was over.

He closed the safe and reset the combination. Then he clambered out of the cupboard and re-stood the ironing board, which seemed very upset at the prospect of remaining in the cupboard and was angry enough to try to fall on his head several more times. The water was now at Humphrey's ankles, so he splashed back to the bedroom finding it more difficult to move fast.

He arrived just in time to catch a glimpse of Jeffrey and Godfrey frantically wiping their mouths (clearly, they had ignored Humphrey's orders to save the biscuits). Humphrey grabbed two pillows, which were still dry, a torch, and a small cylinder of air and shoved them into the ball, then clambered to the top of the wardrobe and reached up to the hatch.

"What are you doing?" asked Godfrey.

"I'm going to open the hatch, then get into the ball, so we can float out when the water lifts us up to the ceiling."

"Won't the water go down?"

"Eventually, but at the moment the water is rising fast. Look... it's almost up to the bed."

Humphrey pulled on the latch, which was far stiffer than he remembered. He pulled and pulled, so hard that his feet were dangling in the air when the latch snapped open and a huge torrent of water fell through it and struck him away with a roar.

"I told you the water will go down," said Godfrey. "You are all wetted now."

Two large, dazed eyes stared through the falling torrent before he was able to half-wade, half-swim his way to the bed. The saturated bear got inside the ball and zip-sealed the entrance just as the water rose over the sheets. A puff of air from the air cylinder inflated the ball and it started to rise with the water.

"It's cold!" yelled Godfrey.

"Yes. The water outside is cold. But we've got the towel and these pillows." Humphrey gave Godfrey and then Jeffrey a good rub down before drying himself. As the water rose the ball rose on top of it, which was when Humphrey realised that the ball was not directly under the escape tunnel.

Then the lights went out and all went pitch black.

"Wah! It's the end of the world!" Godfrey wailed. "I don't want to be end of the worlded!"

"Stop it, Godfrey! You're treading on me," yelled Jeffrey.

"I want to get out! Let me out! Let me out!"

"We're okay, Godfrey, look. I have a torch." Humphrey clicked the torch on, and it lit up under his chin, making him look like an evil and sinister were-bear.

"Wah! There's a monenster in here with us! I don't want to be eatened!"

"Ow! Shdop ib bodvree! You're breading on by head!" There was a slap and Godfrey fell back to land on Humphrey.

"Wah! He hit me! I don't like this game!"

"Here you are, Godfrey, you can hold the torch."

Godfrey snatched at the torch and shone it around and around, frantically checking everyone and looking for the monster were-bear before he calmed down a little.

"I don't like this game. Can we play pirates instead? I like pirates," he sobbed.

The ball spun around the room several times, caught in a current before it stopped at the bottom of the escape tunnel. The bears' secret house was now completely under water and the current had equalised, so the ball rose up the tunnel and popped out onto the surface. The sound of rain pitter-pattered on the ball.

The bears had a few minutes of sightseeing before the ball misted up inside. This was both a good and a bad thing. It was good because any people around would not see a ball of teddy bears gawking at them. It was bad because they could not see where they were drifting to and everything inside the ball was fast becoming damp.

In order to prevent some of their survival supplies from becoming too wet, they finished the biscuits. The stash of spending shortbreads was safe in a water-proof tin, so they decided to save them for later. Well, Humphrey did.

And so it was, that after about twenty minutes or so, Humphrey found himself dozing off on the cold, damp pillows, but with a dry, warm Godfrey curled up asleep on his chest and an almost dry Jeffrey asleep sitting on his legs. They didn't drift very far and were caught at the side of the bridge, on Bridge Road, only a few hundred yards from their home. The gentle pitter-patter of rain helped lull them to sleep.

At about half past six in the morning, they were woken up by blue flashing lights. Jeffrey wiped the inside of the ball and peered out at the police cars blocking the bridge and the officers putting up the 'Road Closed' sign.

Humphrey, from his position at the bottom of the trio, tried to do the same closer to the water line but was startled when he saw another big eye staring back at him. This one was far bigger than the fisheye earlier.

"Dondus!" yelled Godfrey, bouncing up and down in excitement. "Dondus! It's us!"

A big, green reptilian head rose from the water and grinned.

"Dondus! You can play football with us. We're in the ball."

"Uhm... No. Please don't. We're in the ball. Can you nudge us to dry land?"

Dondus' two big nostrils pushed the ball away from the bridge and up beneath a tree. Then he gave it a big bash with his head, and it stuck fast in some of the branches.

"Uhm... Not so helpful, but thanks. I think," called out
Humphrey, wondering how they would avoid people if
anyone cared to look.

The nostrils disappeared and there was a scratching sound on the top.

Jeffrey wiped the inside, and they could just make out Woof, the not-dog that lived in the only beetfruit tree in Godalming.

"Woof! Dondus pushed us to Woof's. Yay!" screamed Godfrey.

"Right!" said Jeffrey who reached up to the zip-seal and pulled.

"Don't do that! It'll deflate the... ahhhh... it's cold!"

Splash!

Luckily Woof was quick to pull the bears out of the water, but now they all needed drying off again.

Woof's tree house is quite small, and the three bears found it quite a challenge to fit in, let alone live there for the several days until the flooding subsided. Woof found it the most challenging – but mainly because woofs like to live alone. Well, that, but also living with The Furricious Gang had its own challenges.

Humphrey was very thankful for his friends, Dondus - Godalming's very own Loch Ness-type monster, and Woof – Godalming's rare tree-dwelling-not-dog-type-thing.

After the flood had eventually subsided it took weeks for their secret home to dry out. They had to pump out the water and then find a way to circulate air around it to remove the damp and unsavoury smells. Everything had to be washed and scrubbed clean and a lot of the rooms had to be redecorated. It was not cheap, and Humphrey had to spend most of his secret slush fund in repairs.

The last project was for Humphrey to build a new emergency watertight chamber, designed to escape from any similar floods in the future. Jeffrey wanted it to be made like a submarine so that they could play snubmanrines in it, but Godfrey wasn't too keen, fearful of monenster were-bears. So, they made it like a spaceship instead, and often play space games in it to this day. It has its own stash of biscuits too – but that always needs refilling after a space game.

Swimming along in the River Wey, as it receded back to its original size, was a very disappointed fish. One of many. Yet again, the promise of a new Great Piscine Empire had failed to materialise. But a few seconds later, as fishes often do, it forgot all about it.

Then, Humphrey remembered something quite disconcerting.

"Uhm... Jeffrey, tell me about those 'Morning After' pills..."

The Furricious Gang

Children's stories for grown ups

Imagine a more fun world where teddy bears really lived in your town, green monsters lived in the rivers, and dog-like woofs lived in trees. That's what these stories are about.

Martyn MacDonald Adams

Martyn lives and works in Godalming. He is a lightly bearded, 1950s vintage guy. For hobbies he likes to play his guitar, compose songs, and write. Despite what the doctors say he assures everyone he is quite sane - although he has been known to wear silly outfits every now and then.

When he gets philosophical, he likes to muse on the fact that we all live together on the crust of a ball of molten rock, whizzing round and around a deadly nuclear fireball while we look up into the sky hoping that nothing bumps into us. Meanwhile, we are poisoning our home and squabbling amongst ourselves for reasons that he completely fails to understand.

ISBN: 978-1-7396924-6-9

9 781739 692469

The Furricious Gang

Of Godalming

Book 3

A children's book for grown ups

Martyn MacDonald Adams